9/12

Ava and the Real Lucille

Cari Best

pictures by

Madeline Valentine

Margaret Ferguson Books

FARRAR STRAUS GIROUX · NEW YORK

For Jose, who saved Bo Peep with a straw —C.B.

To Bob, for getting better —M.V.

Farrar Straus Giroux Books for Young Readers
175 Fifth Avenue, New York 10010

Text copyright © 2012 by Cari Best
Pictures copyright © 2012 by Madeline Valentine
Distributed in Canada by D&M Publishers, Inc.
Color separations by Embassy Graphics Ltd.
Printed in China by Macmillan Production (Asia) Ltd.,
Kwun Tong, Kowloon, Hong Kong (supplier code: 10)
Designed by Roberta Pressel
First edition, 2012
1   3   5   7   9   10   8   6   4   2

mackids.com

Library of Congress Cataloging-in-Publication Data
Best, Cari.
    Ava and the real Lucille / Cari Best ; [illustrated by] Madeline Valentine. — 1st ed.
        p.   cm.
    Summary: Ava and her sister Arlie enter a contest to win a pet but Ava is disappointed
when the pet turns out to be a bird instead of a dog.
    ISBN 978-0-374-39903-0
    [1. Contests—Fiction.   2. Sisters—Fiction.   3. Parakeets—Fiction.   4. Pets—Fiction.]
I. Valentine, Madeline, ill.   II. Title.

PZ7.B46575Av 2012
[E]—dc23
                                                                                           2011031692

Ava saw the sign in the pet store window first, because Arlie, her sister, was tying her tap shoes and Mama was buying strawberries.

Ava's heart jumped. "Now's our chance," she said.

"For what?" asked Arlie.

"To have a dog," said Ava.

"I don't see any D-O-G on the sign," said Arlie.

"We could win a monkey or a llama or a teeny-weeny ant. They're pets, too.

"I want to win a dog," said Ava.

Then, as they were taking baby steps all the way home so Arlie wouldn't ruin her tap shoes, Ava thought of a good beginning to their poem.

"My turn," said Arlie, making up the middle—because she liked dogs, too.

The girls finished the
poem together at Mama's
desk, signed it, made a
copy to keep, folded it into
an envelope, sealed it,
stamped it,

and carried it to the
mailbox on the corner.

"Let's name our dog Lucille," said Ava at dinner.

"Don't count your dinosaurs before they hatch," said Arlie. "Contests are hard to win."

"I think Lucille is a very nice name if she's a girl pet," said Mama. And she gave each of *her* girls a bowl of fresh strawberries with cream for dessert.

"Do you think Mr. Noah will like our poem?" asked Ava
as they got ready for bed.
  "I hope so," said Arlie.
  "Can I hear it?" Mama asked.

"With pleasure," said Ava, and she began to read:

A dog, a dog
A big brown dog
She'll run and splash and play
We'll give her treats
And brush her teeth
And keep the fleas away.
We'll cut her nails
And clean her ears
And love her every day.

"Can't you just smell her?" asked Ava, sniffing with all her might.
"And feel her soft, curly hair?" added Arlie.
"And hear her barking when we come home?" said Ava.

The girls checked the mail every day after school and ran to answer the phone when it rang.

"What's taking so long?" asked Ava after two weeks.

"I guess we didn't win," said Arlie, shrugging her shoulders as she practiced tapping.

But Ava kept hoping. Hoping for a dog just like Feebee next
door. Ava loved how Feebee's ears blew back when she ran;
how her teeth shined white when she smiled; how she danced
when Mr. Alley said, "Feebee, dance!"

Then one day, the phone rang. Ava ran to get it. It was
Mr. Noah.

"Congratulations!" he said. "You and your sister have won
first prize in our 'Write a Poem, Win a Pet!' contest."

"I can't believe we won!" said Arlie.

"I knew it!" said Ava.

"Oh, boy!" said Mama.

A little while later, Mr. Noah appeared at their door behind a big brown box.

"It's Lucille!" shouted Ava, laughing.

Arlie laughed, too.

So did Mama.

Ava and Arlie raced to open the box. They pulled one flap and another. Then two more.

"Let me," begged Ava, wanting to be the first to see Lucille.

"It's a bird," said Ava.
"In a cage!" said Arlie.
"Isn't she beautiful!" said Mr. Noah.
"Indeed!" said Mama.
But Ava didn't think so. Not one bit.

After Mr. Noah left, Arlie said, "You can't give a prize back just because you don't like it."

"Winners can't be losers," said Mama, while she and Arlie looked around for a cozy place to put Lucille.

"Out the window would be perfect," said Ava.

Mama gave Lucille some seeds.

Arlie gave Lucille some water.

Ava gave Lucille a nasty stare. "You're not the real Lucille," she said, narrowing her eyes.

"Squeeeep!" squawked Lucille, and she flew off to the farthest corner of the cage.

"You're scaring her," said Arlie.

"I am not," said Ava.

"Quiet!" said Mama. "It says here that parakeets don't like loud noises."

"Well, neither do I," said Ava, and she stomped her sandals thunderously across the room.

That was the first thing Ava learned about Lucille. But it wasn't the last.

"Why isn't Lucille eating?" asked Arlie the next morning.

"Parakeets don't like big changes," said Mama. "New faces, new colors, new sounds . . ."

"New fingers," said Ava, wiggling her pinkie through a space between two bars.

Then: "Ouch!" said Ava. "I didn't know parakeets had teeth."

"They don't," said Mama. "But they do have sharp beaks."

"Well, I have a sharp tongue," said Ava. And she stuck it out at Lucille. "Why didn't Mr. Noah's sign say 'Write a Poem, Win a Dumb Old Bird'?"

"Lucille can't help being a bird," said Arlie.

"But *you* can help being an impatient Ava," said Mama.

So Ava tried to be patient.

"Lucille looks like a painting," said Arlie between bites of bagel. "She has stripes and squares and dabs and dots."

"And one spot of beige over her beak that tells us she's a girl," said Mama.

"Who sticks to her perch like a magnet sticks to the refrigerator," said Ava, forgetting all about being patient.

One day, while Arlie was practicing for a dance recital and Mama was making strawberry jam, Ava unlatched the door of Lucille's cage.

"Come out!" said Ava. But Lucille didn't.

"Don't you want to play?" asked Ava. But Lucille just sat there.

"Don't be afraid," whispered Ava. But Lucille was.

Ava looked out the window and saw Feebee nosing a
soccer ball.

"I wish I had a—" But before Ava could say "dog,"
something unexpected happened.

It felt like a tickle. Then a nibble. Suddenly a shrieky "Weeet!"
rang out in Ava's ear.

"What was that?" she shouted.

"It's Lucille!" shouted Arlie.

"On your shoulder!" shouted Mama.

"Lucille!" said Ava, laughing.

After that day, Ava discovered that Lucille was full of surprises.

"Look!" she said. "Lucille can watch two things at one time: Mama making a strawberry pie out of her right eye—and me licking the spoon out of her left."

Ava loved when Lucille chirped the second the girls came home from school.

"Weeet!" Ava chirped back.

She was proud when
Lucille rode on *her* finger
to the sink for a shower,

and on *her* pencil top
when she did her math.

Before long, Ava was feeding Lucille, giving her fresh water,
and making sure no cold air blew around her.
"Weeet!" chirped Lucille in appreciation.
"You make our whole house sing," Ava told the little bird.

But Ava and Arlie would never forget the day the house
was silent.

"Weeet!" whistled Ava, but there was no answer.

"Something is very wrong," she said, rushing over to the cage.

There at the bottom Lucille sat huddled, her tiny chest heaving
in and out: "Huh huh huh."

The next day, Lucille didn't eat. She didn't drink.

When Ava asked if they could take Lucille to the vet, Mama said the vet was too expensive.

"Huh huh huh," whispered Lucille.

"We have to help her," said Ava.

"How?" asked Arlie.

"What about Mr. Noah?" asked Mama.

So Ava called him. Mama and Arlie listened in.

"Sounds like Lucille has something like a bird seed stuck in her throat," Mr. Noah said. "You could try floating it out with a straw."

While Mama gently held Lucille, and Arlie stroked her soft, tiny head, Ava let three droplets of water fall into Lucille's mouth and down her throat.

"Whatever's stuck there should be washed away," Ava said, like a vet.

To the fluttering little bird, she said, "Be patient, Lucille. Getting better takes time."

"Huh huh huh," whispered Lucille the next day.

"She's not any better," said Arlie.

"She *will* be," said Ava, hoping hoping hoping while she continued to give Lucille water through a straw.

The next morning, the softest of sounds came from the kitchen. Ava listened. She heard a stronger sound. Then another. "Weeet!" chirped Lucille.

"Weeet!" answered Ava as she went galloping into the kitchen.

Mama and Arlie came running, too. "We're so glad you're back, Lucille!" they shouted.

That Saturday, in a spot of sun, Arlie tapped, Lucille danced, Mama baked, and Ava wrote a poem all by herself. It was called "The Real Lucille."

Lucille, Lucille
Our happy bird
She chirps when we come home
She runs and jumps
And kisses, too
She's ALMOST like a dog
And not a dumb old bird.

In fact, Lucille was so much like a dog,

that Ava could teach her to play a fast game of soccer with a Ping-Pong ball—because Lucille was still full of surprises and Ava had lots of good ideas.